PA'S HARVEST

To Patrick -

A story to call forth your own stories -

April/03

PA'S HARVEST

A TRUE STORY TOLD BY

EPHREM CARRIER

TO

JAN ANDREWS

ILLUSTRATED BY

CYBÈLE YOUNG

A GROUNDWOOD BOOK
DOUGLAS & McINTYRE
TORONTO VANCOUVER BUFFALO

ACKNOWLEDGMENTS

The author wishes to express much gratitude to Ephrem Carrier for the generosity of his collaboration in this book. Thanks are also given to the Writers Reserve Program of the Ontario Arts Council for support, and to Karleen Bradford, Rachna Gilmore, Caroline Parry and Alice Bartels for continuing feedback and friendship.

Groundwood Books / Douglas & McIntyre
720 Bathurst Street, Suite 500, Toronto, Ontario M5S 2R4

Distributed in the USA by Publishers Group West
1700 Fourth Street, Berkeley, CA 94710

We acknowledge the financial support of the Canada Council for the Arts, the Ontario Arts Council and the Government of Canada through the Book Publishing Industry Development Program for our publishing activities.

Canadian Cataloguing in Publication Data

Andrews, Jan, 1942-
Pa's harvest
A Groundwood book.
ISBN 0-88899-405-2
I. Young, Cybèle, 1972- . II. Title.
PS8551.N37P37 2000 jC813'.54 C00-931079-7
PZ7.A52Pa 2000

Printed and bound in China by Everbest Printing Co. Ltd.

To all the storytellers of Canada,

les conteurs du Canada

JA

To Calder

CY

PA'S HARVEST began in the spring. I was too young to think about spring much, but I did know the snow was melting into puddles, and Mom was telling me to keep out of them.

Pa said we had to get started on the potatoes. He took me out with him. He gave me a knife. He didn't even say to be careful.

I sat beside him, working and working. I was wearing my suspenders that were made from the inner tubes of tires. I snapped those suspenders sometimes, just the way he did.

We had to cut the potatoes in halves and quarters. We had to make sure each section had at least one of those little white nobbles he called eyes for seed.

"You cut off their eyes, they won't be able to see when they're down in the earth," he told me.

"Can they really see?" I asked.

The next day I had school, of course. I could only help Pa after I'd come home and had my snack. After I'd

done my other chores, too–filling the woodbox, hauling water, getting the kerosene lamps ready for the night. My brothers were too small for chores like that.

Days and days went by. The potato cutting was over and the chunks stood ready. Pa took me out with him to look at the fields.

"You reckon they're dry enough for plowing?" he asked me.

He waited till I nodded.

Next morning, he hitched up our two horses, King and Bill. He plowed the fields into furrows. When I could, I walked behind him. The earth behind the plow smelled darker. After the plowing was finished, Pa got out the harrow. That was for breaking up the clumps.

"You reckon it's ready for planting?" he asked.

I studied the earth carefully. I nodded once again. He dropped the

chunks of potato into the furrows with the one-row planter. A chunk and a space and another chunk.

I lay in bed in the kitchen at night with my brothers and listened to him telling Mom how he'd bought fertilizer. He told her fertilizer was worth it, but he said the fertilizer cost.

He said sure enough, any day, we'd see those potatoes sprouting. I tried to be patient. He wasn't much better at waiting than I was. Every morning before school he took me to the fields to check. I bent down. I put my eyes close to the ground like he told me.

"There we are," he said.

I saw then there were tiny green

shoots poking up. I went in and I told Mom.

As the days got hotter, the shoots grew into stems and the stems had leaves. Pa had plenty of other work on the farm – he always had work because of the pigs and the cattle and the chickens. We still went to look at the potatoes.

One day there were these small white flowers.

Pa rubbed his hands together. "The best crop ever, this'll be." He put his arm around my shoulders and he squeezed. I felt that squeeze all morn-

ing as I sat in my desk in the front row.

School got out. Pa mounded the potato rows up higher; he weeded and weeded. He called me his helper. I tried to keep up to him but I couldn't.

He started before breakfast every morning. He came into the house in the evenings so Mom had to set supper on the table late. I loved those suppers because while we ate he'd tell us how the potatoes were like money.

"This year, for Christmas, we'll have presents," he'd say to us. "Presents, eh, Mom? Presents from the store."

Summer got done and school started over. I sat in the second row in the classroom now. Cold came in the mornings so I had to dig my hands into my pockets, so I'd see my breath on the air in front of me as I walked.

When we went to the fields, we found the potato plants all blackened.

I wanted to run away but Pa made me put my hand down in the earth. He made me feel around till I found potatoes and potatoes in clusters.

"Didn't I tell you? Lots of them this year." He pulled out a potato and held it up to show me. "We won't just have presents. We'll have clothes, too. New ones."

He squeezed my shoulders even harder. I couldn't imagine it. I'd never had new clothes.

I looked down at my pants and thought how Mom had stitched them out of Pa's old ones. How she was always telling me to be careful so my brothers could have them when I'd grown too much.

I wondered what would happen next. I found out when Pa got the Alphe boys to come over. He took the digger through the fields. The digger turned the potatoes out of the soil so I could see them. There were potatoes all over.

I worked with the Alphe boys putting the potatoes into baskets and

emptying the baskets into barrels. Sometimes I thought my arms would fall off, they hurt so much.

At last the fields were empty and the barrels filled the yard. Pa sat me and my brothers up in a line – a different barrel for each of us. He put his hands around Mom like they might dance.

That night, I heard him tell her how he was going into town tomorrow. I thought of the presents. I

thought of the clothes. I thought of the warm feeling there'd been in the house over supper. I wanted to go with him but Mom said I had school.

After school, when I'd done my chores, I waited for Pa in the kitchen. I listened for him whistling or singing one of his songs. There was the sound of the mare and buggy. Then he was standing in the doorway.

"Everyone's been growing potatoes, seems like. Potatoes aren't selling."

He took the mare and buggy into town the next week and the next week after. He came back and he shrugged. When I went into the yard, I'd see him standing there looking at the barrels like he was counting them. The air was getting even colder. There was ice on the puddles in the mornings.

"We'll have to put the potatoes in the cellar," Pa decided.

He and the Alphe boys made a chute out of sacking. They opened the trap door in the kitchen. They rolled the barrels inside and emptied them out. There was dust on everything. Mom didn't like that.

I tried counting the barrels but there were too many.

"Seven hundred and fifty," Pa said. "Seven hundred and fifty of the best."

He covered the outside cellar door with straw to keep the potatoes from freezing.

"I'll have to go in the woods," he told us.

He hitched up King and Bill and

went away to work at a place called Riley Brook. Mom said it took him two whole days to get there. I wondered if he'd be cold or if he'd have a place to live. I went and sat on the plow where he'd sat. I worried how

maybe – without Mom cooking – he wouldn't get enough to eat.

When I asked what he was doing, Mom said he was cutting down trees. I didn't understand why trees were selling and potatoes weren't.

At Christmas, when he came home, he had this great red beard. He took me to the end of the farm to cut a Christmas tree. He brought it in and set it up so my brothers and I could put on the decorations.

Mom cooked fudge. I smelled it before I even got to the kitchen. Nobody talked about presents. I didn't even want to. I wanted to tell Pa how I'd taken care of the potatoes. How I'd opened the trap door once a week at least so I could look.

He said it was good that I'd done that. He went into town after Christmas with the sleigh. He stayed a long time. When he came back I was almost asleep.

"Maudit!" I heard him say.

I held my breath waiting for Mom to tell him not to swear but she didn't. I heard him talking about how he would have to go in the woods again.

I was afraid something might happen to him. I was afraid he might forget me. Before he went, he reached over and snapped my suspenders. I snapped his.

By the time he came back, the snow was melting again. I'd stopped opening the door to the cellar. There was a funny smell down there. I told

Mom maybe I should have looked after the potatoes better. She said there wasn't anything I could do. Pa took one sniff and went to town.

"I can't even get the price of shipping out of them," he told us.

I didn't understand what he meant. I just knew for the first time I could remember, when he and Mom went to bed, they talked too low for me to hear.

Next morning when I woke up, Pa was already at work. He'd opened the outside cellar doors. He was rolling one of the barrels along a plank to get it to the wagon. There were other barrels waiting. Pa had been filling them back up with potatoes while I was asleep.

He didn't say anything. He just went on, putting barrels on the wagon, until he got to twelve. He tied a rope over and over, across and across the wagon so the barrels were firm.

I thought we'd go down the road.

Instead we crossed the highway. We went into the fields. I wanted to say something about how the potatoes had grown there but I didn't. We went over the railroad tracks. We

went to the bank that dropped into the Saint John River where I wasn't supposed to play. Pa pulled on the reins so King and Bill stopped.

"Come on," he said and set me down.

He climbed back onto the wagon. He rolled one of the barrels to the edge, tipped it and poured the potatoes out. The potatoes thundered down toward the water. When that barrel was empty he got another and another. The barrels were heavy. The potatoes were everywhere, all over the slope. They were floating down the river with the ice chunks.

"Nothing else to do with them, was there?" He had tears in his eyes. I didn't want to look at him. "I couldn't leave them rotting, could I?"

He came and stood beside me.

He gave my shoulders the biggest squeeze of all. We brought two more loads before lunch and two after. I was there with him when he emptied the last barrel.

"Some presents, eh?" he said.

PRESENTS did come. They came later. They weren't what mattered. What mattered was that squeeze. The hard times got harder but always – whether Pa was with us or whether he wasn't – I could feel him in my shoulders giving me strength.

I guess those squeezes were something else Pa planted. I guess they grew even better than the potatoes. I'm all grown up now and I can feel them still.